For George
M.W.

For Samuel
V.A.

First published 1992
by Walker Books Ltd, 87 Vauxhall Walk
London SE11 5HJ

This edition published 1993

Text © 1992 Martin Waddell
Illustrations © 1992 Virginia Austin

The right of Martin Waddell to be identified
as author of this work has been asserted by him in
accordance with the Copyright, Designs and Patents Act 1988

Printed and bound in Singapore by
Tien Wah Press (Pte.) Ltd

British Library Cataloguing in Publication Data
A catalogue record for this book is
available from the British Library.
ISBN 0-7445-3212-4

Sailor Bear

Written by
Martin Waddell

Illustrated by
Virginia Austin

WALKER BOOKS
LONDON

Small Bear was a bear
in a sailor suit
who was lost
and had no one to play with.
"Now what shall I do?"
wondered Small Bear.

He thought and he thought,
then he looked at his suit
and he *knew* what to do.

"I'll be a sailor, and sail on the sea!"
  decided Small Bear.
  But he hadn't a boat.
"Now what shall I do?"
  wondered Small Bear.

He thought and he thought,
  then he looked at the sea
  and he *knew* what to do.

"I'll go and get one!"
decided Small Bear.
He went to the harbour
but the boats there
were too big for a bear.
"Now what shall I do?"
wondered Small Bear.

He thought and he thought,
then he looked round the shore
and he *knew* what to do.

"Small bears need small boats,
so I'll make one!"
decided Small Bear.
He made a boat
from some pieces of wood
and half a barrel.
He called it "Bear's Boat"
and he took it down to the sea.
BUT...

the sea looked too big for his boat.
"Now what shall I do?" wondered Small Bear.

He thought and he thought, then he looked
at a puddle and he *knew* what to do.

"Small boats need small seas,
so I'll find one!"
decided Small Bear.
He went to the park
where he found a small sea
AND...

Small Bear sailed in "Bear's Boat

...y the light of the moon. BUT...

the sea grew too rough! "Bear's Boat" rocke

nd it rolled and it shattered and SANK!

Small Bear swam and swam till he reached the shor

where he lay on a rock all shivering and cold.

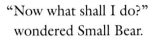

"Now what shall I do?"
wondered Small Bear.

He thought and he thought,
then he sighed at the moon
for he didn't know what to do!
"I'm sick of the sea
so I think I'll give up!"
decided Small Bear with a sniff.
He curled up by the rock
and went sadly to sleep all alone.

The very next morning a little girl
came and she found Small Bear
and she hugged him
and took him home
and set him to dry by the fire.
"Now what shall I do?"
wondered Small Bear.

He thought and he thought,
then he looked at the girl
and he *knew* what to do.

"I'm FOUND,
   and I've someone to play with,
   so I'll stay where I am!"
   decided Small Bear,
   and he cuddled up
   close to the girl
   and he stayed...

… and he never went back to the sea!